ANURAKTHI

A PASSIONATE LOVE STORY

KADARI LINGASWAMY

ISBN 979-888546426-0

I dedicate this story to everyone who has heart to love other person and people who dream for best love story. Love is endless but people changes and love is age less but their presentation differs. This is a pleasant feel good love story with suspense. I hope you all love it.

THANKYOU

KLS

Contents

Foreword

The first writer i know was me. I never aspire to become writer but my love towards fantasy and stories made me to start write skits. I wrote few stage plays in my school and encouragement from my teachers and friends boosted my confidence that i can write .I stopped writing after my 12th standard because of academics but somehow destiny made me to write a story after so many years and that too a love story. I have so many fantasy love stories but genuine story telling feels you that is not a fantasy. Sometimes you must travel into a fantasy world to forget your pains and problems for some time. This is my attempt and i hope you will love and encourage.

Preface

I believe that their is only one story but point of view changes from person to person and situation made them behave different and their character leads them a different destiny.Some of the incidents in this story feels you similar to your life or adapted from some movie scene.But i hope you will feel fresh and intruging.

This is a story of an independet girl PRIYA subramanyam who is known for her character and beauty.A girl or boy feels love some or the other time at any age.We will see how destiny helped priya to find her love.

THANKYOU

KADAR.LINGASWAMY

Acknowledgements

This is purely a fictional story with fictional characters. This story and characters are not derived or based on any events or persons.

I sincerely apologize for anything which made you feel bad as it is own ideological story so it may differ with your thoughts. It is a genuine and sensible story with human emotions and good narration.

I have to thank all the people who encouraged me to develop from a layman to skilled writer .I thank my family, friends Kranthi, Kaushik, Paveena, Manish, Srikar, Dileep and special thanks to Haritha dhi, kalyani dhi all my readers who supported and encouraged me and last but most important thanks for NOTION PRESS founders for full-filling dreams of so many aspiring writers.

THNKYOU ALL.

Prologue

Love happens accidentally and it might happen with anyone and anywhere .Love gives you beautiful memories in your life. Priya is a unique girl and have different prospective on love and does not believe in destiny. But she fell in love with someone whom she never met and never saw before. This story is perfect example of love which does not need of good looks or money but the good heart and good thoughts. What made priya to believe in destiny and how she fell in love? TO KNOW , HOW? WHY? WHEN?

Please read complete story and support me.

ANURAKTI

---A passionate love story

KLS Creations

INTRODUCTION

PRIYA

Hi! everyone,my name is priya subramanyam.I am an independent girl.I am 20 years young.I am a beautiful girl.Yes beautiful! people who come to propose me say this thing.

Today also i got a love letter and a small boy delievered it to me.He said someone gave this greeting card and a letter to him and told him to deliver them to me.I simply tore the card and retuned to the boy and said i didnot believe in love .

CHAPTER ONE

MY DREAM JOB

After a few days.....

I am searching for a good job and applied for all the jobs which matches with my qualifications and today i got a call letter from an MNC company called DEV.Int.Pvt Ltd.I am very happy because this is a dream job and in a reputed company. I cannot expect anything more today.I have to report in the company in next week.

I was eager to join in job and i was literally wanting to sun rise earlier and sets earlier everyday.Finally thc day comes and i joined my job.It is very healthy atmosphere here and all my colleagues became good friends.

Days are passing very fast or may be i am feeling it because of good time.

Today i got a mail from my MD and summary of it was appreciating for my work and at end he wrote he is giving a prestigious project with believe and congratulated me for that.

Next day i was called to meet MD in his cabin .I met my MD and he explained me about project details and he said that i should work in manglore for six months on this project.

CHAPTER TWO

MY life in Manglore

I landed in Manglore city and it is wonderful and specially beach looks lovely.I got a room with the help of a local friend .I entered into the room and it is dusty and dark.I switched on the lights .Room was well equiped and it was artistic with paintings and quotes.I called the owner to send someone to clean the room.I waited for sometime and no one came.I cleaned the room myself.

Enter Caption

The room was full of pintings and quotes on friendship,love,life.I felt that previous tenant was artistic person and then i saw letter on the desk.I felt not to pickup but this atmosphere encouraged me to pickup the letter and i opend it and started reading letter.

Enter Caption

Hi! My dear friend .I am tenant here and staying from few days and i love this place .I spent most of my time in the last few days here.I hope you too love this place .I have two friends here first one is moksha ita sparrow which comes to meet me in the evenings and i will offer her some grains and water at my window.Second one is BIO a rare plant .You will be thinking why i am saying all these things .I wanted you to take care of them atleast for fewdays until i return .I donot know you and you donot know me but i hoping you will accept my request.

Thankyou...

David Harish.

It is weird .How can someone write letter to someone whom you donot know ?

(I questioned myself).But i felt request is reasonable so i decided to do according to his request.

i am feeling like days are passing very fast in manglore may because i am enjoying here and especially this room near beach and with Moksha and Bio.

Enter Caption

CHAPTER THREE

THE UNKOWN PERSON

I am getting ready for the job. I heard someone is knocking the door. A person is in front of the door. He asked for a person called David Harish .I said, no! David is not here. I am a new tenant in this room .He gave his phone number and requested to call him when he returns. He was about to leave and i called him inside and offered him tea. I called him inside because i wanted to figure out who is David Harish. He looks very interesting character for me.

I asked who are you and what is your? Why did you want to meet Harish?

He replied my name is Ranjith. Harish changed my life .I asked him to explain clearly.

I was a thief .One day i robbed a house and returning a vehicle dashed me and went away. I was injured and fell unconscious when i got up i was in the house which i robed last night. I was afraid but a man came to me and said to relax .I was puzzled and seeing my face he smiled. He said do not worry i will explain. You came to my house last night from top of the roof and i was aware of that and i wanted to see how a thief robs .I was anxious and followed you from my house and you met with accident.

I was in uncomfortable situation and i put my hand in pocket to return his money back. He took it back and commented nothing. I was little disappointed of returning money but his gesture made me happy. He told me to take rest till evening.

In the evening he took me to the temple i thought he is spiritual but later he showed me a beggar who was donating his money in hundi. He is Raman and he will beg for whole day and in evening he took the money he required and donates remaining amount to orphanage.

Enter Caption

Then on the way we stopped at a tea stall near to factory. He showed an old man was having his tea .He is kareem working hard at the age of 60 not for his children or for his family. He adopted two children who lost their parents in an accident.

Then finally we went to an orphanage .We met few children who does not have parents or relatives and we met few physically and mentally challenged children. We spent some time there and returned to room.

He told me these people chose to live for others even their situation is worse. "life is not which you live for yourself but life is something which we live with others". Some will leave for their children, parents, country. One should find the reason for their life as human.

He gave me 10,000 rupees and asked me not to rob any house for a week. He told me to use this money to live and start a new life. He asked me to think once about his life. After his words, I realized my mistakes and change my mind. I used only 2000 from it and donated the remaining amount to the orphanage. I started working in a factory and helping others.

But after that day I was busy with my work and not able to meet him , today i came to meet and thank him for everything.Thank you for your tea. I have some work please call me when Harish Returns.

CHAPTER FOUR

Is HARISH dead? or alive?

Ranjith speaks to Priya. I got information about Harish. One of my friends told me that he had seen Harish in an orphanage.so, I came here to meet him if possible you can meet him here or know about him. I said, ok! He left the room. I started thinking about the person. He is a great person. We find only a few who can inspire people. If possible I should meet him once before leaving for Hyderabad. Days are passing and no clue about Harish. It's already 6 months since I have to go to Hyderabad in a few days and I thought I can't meet him.

Suddenly, I received a call from Ranjith.

I told Ranjith that If he finds Harish, please call me. I too want to meet him once. so, he called me.

Ranjith speaks to Priya. I got information about Harish. One of my friends told me that he had seen Harish in an orphanage.so, I came here to meet him if possible you can meet him here or know about him.

I went into the orphanage and visited the church in orphan but Ranjith has to go urgently so he said to me to continue and give an update about Harish by the call.

Enter Caption

I went into the orphanage and visited Church in an orphanage. I met mother ESA. I asked her did she know about David harshly? she replied, yes I know him. He comes here regularly. He donated some amount to the orphanage. He is a good person and a great human being. I asked the mother, where can I meet him? mother asked who are you? Why did you want to meet him? I told them I am an old friend of his and not in touch with him.

Mother ESA, ok. He is not alive. He passed away a year back.

CHAPTER FIVE

DAVID HARISH'S death mistery.

I am shocked, how can it be possible Ranjith told me he was seen 3 months backs. But Mother is saying he is dead a year back.

Enter Caption

I asked the mother for his latest photo of him. The mother gave me one picture.

I took a picture and sent it to the Ranjith. Ranjith called me. Priya who is this person and why did you send me?

I said, he is Mr.David Harish. Mother ESA gave me this picture.

He replied, he is not David Harish. I am surprised and confused. What! How can it be possible? I got this from the orphanage and mother ESA also told Harish is dead a year.

He asked, How it is possible? My friend recognizes Harish and why he will give the wrong information to me. We are confused and who is this person?

CHAPTER SIX

Person in the PHOTO

Days are passing no clue about Harish and now it's time to return me home. I am feeling sad that I couldn't find Harish. I have packed my bags. I have a flight tomorrow and i am hoping to find something about Harish.

I landed in Hyderabad. I submitted my work to my boss and he appreciated me for my work.

MY boss told me you have to meet the director in his cabin with my colleague. I and my colleague both went to meet the director in his cabin.

For the first time, I am meeting my director. I entered the cabin with some nervous but he appreciated me for my work in the Mangalore project.

I saw a photo in the director's cabin. I am new to this job so I asked my colleague about the person in photo. My colleague replied he is Kalyan Dev son of Ramesh Dev director of Dev international private limited. He worked here for a few days and now he is in Europe.

Days are passing and rainy season. Trees are green everywhere and looking beautiful. I am remembering my days in Bangalore with Moksha ,Bio and Harish. I was also dissapointed that not able to meet Harish.

CHAPTER SEVEN

The Photo in my director's house

After a few days...

My boss called me and told me to meet the director at his house with the files. I am feeling nervous because it was not a formal meet. I went to the director's house and rang the bell.

A person opened the door. I said I am here to meet the director. He offered me a coffee and said to wait for him. I am having my coffee and unfortunately, I drop some coffee on my dress. He showed me a room and said to please clean yourself.

I said ok and went into the room. Room is beautiful and I clean myself. I am coming outside the room. Suddenly my eyes dropped on a photo on the wall and I am shocked after seeing the photo.

This person photos in this house. I am confused and eager after seeing the photo in the house. I went into the hall and met the director. I am physically in front of him but my mind is somewhere. I completed my meeting with the director.I want to know about the picture in the room. So i asked my director about the picture and he said, he is my son Kalyan Dev and his friend.

CHAPTER EIGHT

ASTONISHING truth!

I returned to my house . I opened my bag and removed a diary from the bag. I have bought this dairy from my director's house from the room where I saw the photo.

Enter Caption

I opened the diary and read the diary completely and I am amazed after the reading diary.

I got some information and decided to go to Mangalore again. I reached Mangalore and called Ranjith. I show a picture which I saw in the director's room.

Priya from where did you get this photo?

I asked do you know these people? He said I know one of them.

I asked who is he?

Ranjith replied he is David Harish, whom we are searching and another one is in the picture which you sent me on that day and told me he is Mr. David Harish.

Did you find anything Priya? Where did you get this picture?

I am surprised because he is saying Kalyan is David Harish.

Priya please tell me what do you get to know about Harish?

I am in shock, so after a few minutes, I explained him. Kalyan Dev and David Harish are in the picture. The David Harish you know is not him. He is Kalyan Dev, s/o Ramesh Dev director of Dev international private limited. I am working in Dev international and one day I saw this picture in my director's house. I get to know Kalyan dev and David Harish are best friends from Ramesh Dev. I found a diary from his house.

CHAPTER NINE

The DIARY

Who is diary it is?

That diary belongs to David Harish.

He is an orphan. He is a Gallivant and he loves to help others. His only best friend is Kalyan Dev. He travels almost 365 days in a year except a week, that week he comes to Hyderabad to spend time with Kalyan Dev. But Harish died of blood cancer a year back. He has a last wish, which he wants to full-filled by his friend but he does not want to tell Kalyan Dev about his blood cancer. His last wish is difficult to fulfill by Kalyan Dev .I feel Kalyan Dev read the diary and left his aHome to full-fill his friend's last wish.

I want to confirm this so I wanted to visit an orphanage and ask my mother essay about Kalyan.I and Ranjith went into an orphanage and. met mother Esa.

I asked mother Esa by showing the photo, Do you know this person? She replied, yes he is Harrish and his friend David Harish.

We Understood that Kalyan Dev is acting or living the life of David Harish.

CHAPTER TEN

Ramesh Dev's confession

Priya, now what do you want to do?

He left his house for his friend.(I am thinking about Kalyan in my mind)

I too don't know but want to meet him at least once after knowing all these things.

I came back to Hyderabad. I met Ramesh Dev and asked about Kalyan Dev.

Ha, priya what do you want to know about my son and why?

Sir everyone is saying your son is in Europe but is it true?

Yes, he is in Europe.

No sir, he is not in Europe, he left his house to fulfill his friend's last wish you know this.

Yes, But I can't say these things to the outside world. We too are worried about him. But we can't find him anywhere.

Sorry Sir, I came to know about your son from the diary which I found in your house.If possible i will find him and inform you.

CHAPTER ELEVEN

In search of Kalyan

After a few days.....

Why I am thinking so much about Kalyan after knowing the truth? Why I want to meet him? Am I loving him? Everything is a question for me now about Kalyan. I know only one thing that he became an important person in my life .I decided to find him and wanted to find answers to all my questions. I read David Harish's diary and I got to know David Harish will visit Kailashnathar temple in Kanchipuram every year. So I feel Kalyan will also go there. May be I can find him there and the day comes when David Harish will go to the temple every year.

Enter Caption

I went to the temple and started searching for the Kalyan but I can't find him anywhere so I try to enquire all the people by showing his photo. Someone recognized him and said he didnot came to the temple this time but you can find him in Varanasi.

CHAPTER TWELVE

UNKOWN FEELINGS

I did not find Kalyan but i got some information about Kalyan. I started feeling something for him but I didn't know, what is that feeling? It is new to me I always feel this when I am listening the name of Kalyan. My heart is beating fast when I am searching for Kalyan may be this love. I am started loving him.

Enter Caption

I want to express my love to him, but I should meet him first so i decided to go to varanasi. I reached Varanasi and start searching for Kalyan I am feeling my two eyes are not enough to search for him because I am desperate to meet him. Then I saw a few children are playing and one man is playing with them.

I got tired in searching of him and sat there. I started to watch their play. I saw Kalyan with them. The man who is playing with children is Kalyan.

I am trying to move but I am frozen in that place for a moment. I am fully emotional now but I am trying to control my emotions.

I went there and met Kalyan. I introduced myself as Ranjith's friend. I started talking casually with him.

We had a conversation there. I Said, I am searching for you.

Ok! Priya why you are searching for me?

I need your help I want you to come with me to Hyderabad to meet a person.

Ok, who is the person can I know?

Sorry, Kalyan, I can't say you now but you should come with me. Kalyan accepted to come.

CHAPTER THIRTEEN

BACK TO HYD

I reached Hyderabad. I took him to his house. He is shocked and began to look at my face. I handed the diary to him and we met his parents. I left him in his house and returned home.

I am happy today that atleast I finally found Kalyan. I want to express my feelings to Kalyan but felt this is not the correct time.

After a few days...

I wanted to express my love to him. So I wanted to talk to him and went to his house.

I met Ramesh Dev and asked sir if Kalyan is at home?

No, he left the house after two days when you bring him here.

Listening to Ramesh Dev I felt depressed. I went to his room and sat in his room.

I am started thinking about myself. In the last few days, my life has become adventurous and few people become important in my life.

CHAPTER FOURTEEN

EMOTIONAL ROLLER COASTER

Suddenly, I saw a room is opened inside the Kalyan room. I went to the door and opened it. It was dark and dusty. I switched on the lights. After seeing the room my heartbeat is stopped for a moment and I became fully emotional. My eyes are filled with tears.

Enter Caption

I am shocked because the room is full of my photos on the walls. I can't stop myself from feeling emotional I start searching for something and I found a greeting card from the drawer. I felt I have seen this greeting card somewhere. I am not able to remember.

The greeting was torn and it is joined with gum. I saw this card somewhere and this was for me. I remembered, one day a boy came to me with this greeting card. I tore this card and returned it to him.

I am more emotional now. I felt that, I love Kalyan and wanted to express my love for him but now I found he loves me more than me.

CHAPTER FIFTEEN

CLIMAX

I am now desperate to meet Kalyan but thinking where can I find him?

Suddenly my phone rang, it was Ranjith.

Hi Priya, I am Ranjith and I have something about Kalyan. He returns to Mangalore and he is in his room.

I ended the call next sec and took the next flight to Mangalore.

I reached Mangalore and went straight to the room. I knocked the door and Kalyan opens the door and welcome me inside.

I went inside and hug him tightly for some time. I am out of control now and I can't stop my emotions anymore. Kalyan was silent and I was speechless but may be he understood my emotions with my hug.

I am now normal after becoming so emotional. I bent on my knee and proposed to him. I said do you want to marry me? He took a moment and said yes!

He asked Priya do you love Kalyan or Harish?

I love both of them because both are you. I love your heart and character.

May be i rejected you unknowingly but now I am loving you knowingly.We got married and we started a new life.

Enter Caption

Story Theme

Kalyan remembers one thing said by someone "eventually you will end up where you need to be, with whom you are meant to be with and doing what you should do we doing".

I can’t say this is the end of the story because every ending is the possibility of a new beginning.

Enter Caption

Life is like a cyclic process, some moments are beginning for someone and it is ending for someone.

THANK YOU FOR READING

K-L-S

9 798885 464260

Printed by Libri Plureos GmbH in Hamburg,
Germany